A modern appro

CU00842101

Reading and writing
natural activities and
next most important
designed to stimulate and interest him and to
give daily practice at the right level.

Educational experts from five Caribbean countries have co-operated with the author to design
and produce this Ladybird Sunstart Reading
Scheme. Their work has been influenced by (a)
the widely accepted piece of research *Key
Words to Literacy*[1], a word list which is
adapted here for tropical countries and used to
accelerate learning in the early stages; and (b)
the work of Dr. Dennis Craig[2] of the School of
Education, U.W.I., and other specialists who
have carried out research in areas where the
English language is being taught to young
children whose natural speech on entering
school is a patois or dialect varying consider-
ably from standard English.

[1] Key Words to Literacy *by J McNally and W Murray,
    published by The Teacher Publishing Co Ltd,
    Derbyshire House, Kettering, Northants, England.*

[2] An experiment in teaching English *by Dennis R Craig,
    Caribbean Universities Press, also* Torch *(Vol. 22, No. 2),
    Journal of the Ministry of Education, Jamaica.*

THE LADYBIRD SUNSTART READING SCHEME consists of six books and three workbooks. These are graded and written with a controlled vocabulary and plentiful repetition. They are fully illustrated.

Book 1 'Lucky dip' (for beginners) is followed by Book 2 'On the beach'. Workbook A is parallel to these and covers the vocabulary of both books. The workbook reinforces the words learned in the readers, teaches handwriting and introduces phonic training.

Book 3 'The kite' and Book 4 'Animals, birds and fish' follow Books 1 and 2, and are supported by Workbook B. This reinforces the vocabulary of Books 3 and 4 and again contains handwriting exercises and phonic training.

Book 5 'I wish' and Book 6 'Guess what?' with Workbook C complete the scheme.

The illustrated handbook (free) for parents and teachers is entitled 'A Guide to the Teaching of Reading'.

For classroom use there are two boxes of large flash cards which cover the first three books.

BOOK 6
The Ladybird SUNSTART Reading Scheme
(a 'Key Words' Reading Scheme)

Guess what?

by W. MURRAY
with illustrations by MARTIN AITCHISON

Ladybird Books Loughborough
in collaboration with Longman Caribbean

The library

Most children like to read books. Some boys and girls can borrow books from school to read at home. Many borrow books from a library.

Joy and her friend Lyn borrow books from a library. Sometimes they talk about the

books they like best. One day, on their way to the library, Joy says to Lyn, "I like story books best. I like a true story about people like us, but who have an adventure."

"Yes," says Lyn. "I like story books. But best of all I like a book that tells me how to do things and how to make things."

Ken and Ray come along. They walk with the girls as they are all going to the library. Ray tells them that he wants to find a book about fishing and fishing boats.

Ken knows about a book called *Our Wonderful World*. He wants to borrow it. "I think it's just the kind of book I like best," he says. "It is not a story book. It is all true."

The children see more of their friends. Barry, Gail, Dave and Sandra are going into the library.

Our wonderful world

The children talk to their friends and then look at books in the library.

Lyn borrows two books to take away. One is *Make Your Own Magic*, and the other *Fun and Games at Home*. Joy takes out a story book about adventures at sea. Ray has a book called *A First Book on Fishing*.

Ken finds *Our Wonderful World*, the book he wants to borrow. There is much to read in it, but there are many pictures as well.

Ken sees in his book a picture of the outside of the earth, and then one of the inside of the earth. On the outside there are the seas, and the lands where people live.

He reads that deep inside the earth are rock and metal. The rock and metal are so very hot that they have melted. Sometimes some of the melted rock and metal from inside the earth comes out on to the land or into the sea. This is dangerous for people who live near. At times some of them are killed.

is very hot inside the earth

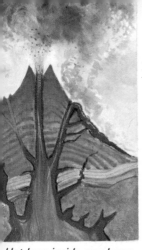

Hot lava inside a volcano

A volcano

Ken reads that when some of the very hot melted rock and metal comes from inside the earth, it is called lava. This lava comes out through a volcano. A volcano is an opening in the outside or surface of the earth.

A picture shows some of the melted rock and metal as it comes out of the volcano. The hot lava cools when it comes out. This takes some time.

As the lava cools on the surface of the earth it goes hard. If much more lava comes out, cools and gets hard, it can make a mountain. Sometimes, when there is a volcano under the sea, it can make an island in the sea. After a very long time, when things grow on it, people can live on the island. There are many islands that have come from volcanoes. Some of these are very beautiful now, and many people live on them.

Ken's friends tell him that it is time to go home. He takes the book with him, as he wants to read more.

Hot springs from the earth

Ken reads more of his book at home and shows it to his friends. Here are some of the things they find out from it.

A spring is water that comes up through an opening in the surface of the earth. Sometimes the water from a spring is hot. There are many countries in the world where there are hot springs which come from inside the earth.

The water of a hot spring has been heated by the hot rock deep down under the surface. Many hot springs are near a volcano, or near a place where a volcano used to be. Volcanoes are not all in hot countries.

Hot water pipes in Reykjavik, Iceland, carry water from natural hot springs to heat most of the houses.

This picture is from an island country where there is ice and snow. There have been volcanoes and now there are many hot springs. The people make much use of the hot springs in that country. They take the heated water from the hot springs to their houses in large pipes. The picture shows one of these large pipes, and some children going along it.

An earthquake

Sometimes a part of the surface of the earth shakes. This is called an earthquake. An earthquake happens because of the great heat inside the earth. This heat can make the hard rocks near the surface move and shake.

Earthquakes happen on most days, in one part of the world or another. But most earthquakes are under the sea, and not many of them do damage.

Some earthquakes kill people and damage buildings. A few have killed many people, and have damaged many buildings.

One picture in Ken's book shows what can happen in an earthquake. In it some houses and other buildings are being damaged and some people fall down an opening in the earth.

Another picture shows the world and the parts of it where there are most earthquakes. Most of these places are near the sea.

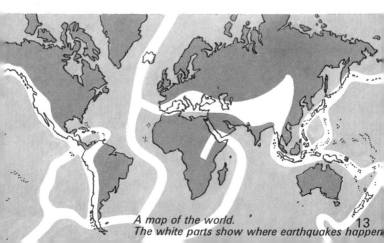

A map of the world.
The white parts show where earthquakes happen

13

Coral

Ken sees that his book *Our Wonderful World* has some pictures of coral, and things made from it. It says in the book that an island can be made from coral. He has read an adventure book called *Coral Island*, which he liked. He now reads that there are many islands made from coral. It makes him want to know more about coral.

As he reads on, he learns that coral is something like rock and is made from the skeletons of tiny animals that live in the sea. There are very many of these tiny skeletons that go to make up a little coral. But coral can grow to be very large with more and more of the tiny skeletons added to it over a great many years.

There are different kinds of coral. Some of them are coloured. The colours can be beautiful. Where there are coloured corals in the sea, at times it can look like a beautiful garden under the water.

Coral is made from the skeletons of many millions of tiny jelly-like creatures called Coral Polyps which grow in warm seas

These beads are made from coral ▶

The Sea Gardens

Many people come to look at these beautiful Sea Gardens, as they are called. Coral grows only where the sun is hot. The tiny animals which make coral can live only in warm seas. Some people like to go into the warm sea where it is not very deep, and swim under the water to look at the Sea Gardens.

Others see the Sea Gardens from a boat as they look down on them through the water. A few boats have glass bottoms. People in these boats can see the different coloured corals and the beautiful fish through the glass bottoms. Some say that the coloured fish look like butterflies in the Sea Gardens.

As it is hot where there are coral islands, things grow very well on them. People who live there are lucky to live in the sun by the sea in these beautiful places.

Looking down through a glass-bottomed boat at the Sea Gardens in the Bahamas

Eels

Ray has read his book about fishing. He now knows a lot about fish and about eels.

An eel is a kind of fish which looks something like a snake. It can be small, or big, or very large. It can live in the sea or a river. Men catch some kinds of eels to eat.

In the part of the world near the Atlantic Ocean, the mother eels swim from the rivers in different countries through the Atlantic Ocean to the Sargasso Sea. The Sargasso Sea is part of the Atlantic Ocean. The mother eels lay their eggs in the Sargasso Sea, which has much seaweed in it. They lay their eggs in the seaweed.

Then the little eels from the eggs swim through the Atlantic Ocean to the rivers of the different countries near the Atlantic. They grow as they swim. It can take them years to get there.

After some years in the rivers, the eels swim back to the Sargasso Sea, where the mother eels lay their eggs. This happens year after year.

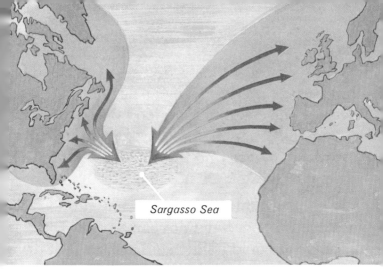

Sargasso Sea

All the Common Eels of North America, Great Britain and other countries of Europe come from the Sargasso Sea

The Common Eel

19

Stories of the Sargasso Sea

The name Sargasso Sea means the sea of seaweed. There is so much seaweed in this very large sea that for a long time stories were told about it. There were many different stories and they all told of danger. Most of these were not true.

It was said that if a ship went into the Sargasso Sea, it did not come back. The seaweed could hold a ship fast, so that it could not move again. It was said that very big and dangerous animals lived on large islands of seaweed. These could get on a ship and kill the men on it. The stories told of sunken ships and the skeletons of many men at the bottom of the deep Sargasso Sea.

We now know that ships can go through the Sargasso Sea with no danger from the seaweed. The seaweed does not stop a ship. There are no large animals on the seaweed, only very tiny ones.

There are no rocks there, no islands, and no land of any kind.

Christopher Columbus

In the year 1492 Christopher Columbus and his men sailed from Spain to the west. After a hard and dangerous time they got to what we now know as the West Indies. They were the first to do this. It is said that they sailed through the Sargasso Sea on the way to the West Indies.

Christopher Columbus wanted to find India. He did not find India, but he thought he had, when he came to the West Indies. This is why the West Indies are so named. When he sailed back to Spain he said that he had been to India. He thought he had, and the people of Spain thought he had.

Christopher Columbus and his men wanted to get more land for Spain, and to find gold and other treasures to take back to Spain. He did this, and after a few years people from Spain and other countries sailed over the Atlantic Ocean to live in the West Indies and America.

Most people now think that Christopher Columbus was a great man. There are many books which tell more about him.

Columbus thought that the world was round, when many did not think so. He said, "Sail to the West, and shall the East be found."

23

The Kaieteur Falls

Joy has been to the library again. She now has a different book. It is about her own country and other countries near it. She reads about Guyana and the great Kaieteur waterfalls there.

The land of Guyana has many rivers and waterfalls. Most people know that the beautiful Kaieteur Falls are much higher than the Niagara Falls. The fall of water of Kaieteur is five times that of Niagara.

To see the wonderful Kaieteur Falls you can fly over them, but it is best to walk up on to the Kaieteur cliffs. Then, when you look over the cliffs, you can hear the great sound and see the fall of the white water so far down into the great pool at the bottom, by the black rocks.

Niagara Falls

Old Man's Falls is another name for these great falls. It comes from an old story about an Indian who was killed when he went over the falls into the pool at the bottom.

Joy tells her friend Lyn that she would like to go to Guyana and the other countries the book tells about.

The Kaieteur Falls of Guyana are five times higher than the Niagara Falls of North America

Kaieteur Falls

25

Men get asphalt from the Pitch Lake, Trinidad

The Pitch Lake of Trinidad

Joy reads on in her book, and learns more.

Joy has seen men use asphalt as they make a road surface. We have all seen this. Joy reads that this asphalt has come from Trinidad.

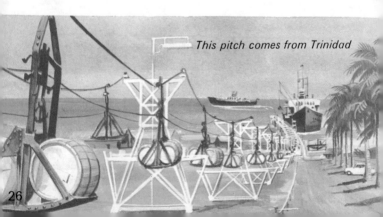
This pitch comes from Trinidad

In Trinidad there is a great lake of asphalt. It is called the Pitch Lake. Pitch is natural asphalt and this asphalt in Trinidad has not been made by man. It just comes up out of the earth.

Some of this natural asphalt or pitch is used on the roads and buildings of Trinidad, but most of it goes to other parts of the world. Much goes to America and Britain.

The pitch is dark in colour and when it is cold it is hard. It melts when made hot. When men use the pitch or asphalt on roads or buildings they first make it hot. When they have put it down it cools and goes hard. Pitch will not let water go through it.

Workmen using asphalt on a road

An old story about the Pitch Lake of Trinidad

There is an old story of an Indian village which sank down into the Pitch Lake of Trinidad. It is said that long, long ago some Indians had a fight. The Indians who won, made a village where the Pitch Lake is now. Then the Indians who had won the fight had a dance. They used coloured feathers when they dressed up for the dance. To get the feathers they killed some humming birds.

These Indians worshipped what they called The Great Spirit. This Great Spirit they worshipped did not like to see the beautiful little humming birds killed. The Great Spirit was angry about this. To show that he was angry, he made the village sink into the earth. From that time long ago, so the story goes, there has always been pitch in the place where the village sank.

Aluminium from bauxite

Lyn finds a different book. Here is something she reads.

Aluminium is one of the most used metals in the world. It is sometimes called the "Magic Metal" because it has so very many uses. Where people are, there you will find aluminium being used. Aluminium is light but strong. It is not hard to work with, and it does not rust.

You cannot find natural aluminium in the earth, as you can find gold or some other metals. It has to be made from bauxite. Bauxite is something like rock. There is bauxite in the West Indies. Much of this is found in Jamaica.

A lot of the bauxite in Jamaica goes to America to be made into aluminium. At first the aluminium is soft. Soft aluminium has not many uses, so other metals are added to it to make it hard.

Then the things that are made from the hard aluminium go all over the world. Most people like the look of aluminium. They also like things made of it, because they are strong, light and do not rust.

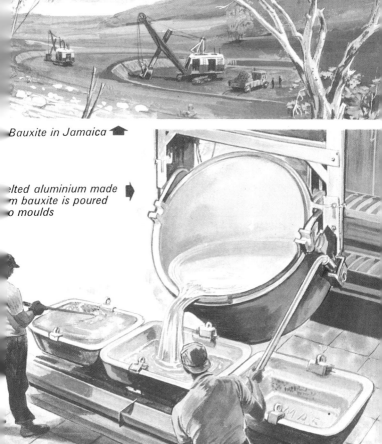

Bauxite in Jamaica

Melted aluminium made from bauxite is poured into moulds

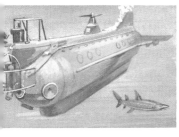

Some things made from aluminium

*A footprint of a dinosaur made millions of years a
It was made in mud, which is now as hard as roc*

The footprint of a dinosaur

Millions of years ago, long before there were any men, huge animals lived here on earth. Some of these huge animals were the dinosaurs. There were many kinds of dinosaurs, and they lived on the earth for millions of years.

The dinosaur was much larger than any animal that lives on land now. A man would look very small beside a dinosaur.

We know that the dinosaurs were huge, as a few skeletons of them have been found. We have also found a huge footprint of a dinosaur. There is a good picture of this footprint, which shows how big it is. There is a pool of water in the footprint and a small boy is in the water, in the footprint.

How is it that the footprint is here now? In the first place the dinosaur must have made it in something soft. Then this got hard, and as the years went by, it got harder and harder. Now it is as hard as rock.

Who? What? When? Where? How? Why?

All children ask questions. It is a good way to learn. They are always asking questions like Who? What? When? Where? How? Why? Many people help them with answers to their questions, but no one knows all the answers.

One good way to find out the answers to questions is to use an encyclopedia. The girl at the library shows the children an encyclopedia and how to use the books.

She tells them that an encyclopedia is a collection of man's knowledge. No one man or woman could write all of an encyclopedia. Many people's knowledge makes up the collection.

You look up what you want to know in the index. An index is a list of everything in the collection. You have to know your a, b, c, to find what you want in the index or list. When you find it, it tells you in which book to look, and on which page. You find the book and the page, and there is the answer you want. If you are lucky, there will also be a picture to help you.

You have to know the alphabet to use an index

A microscope

Ken and Dave use an encyclopedia to find out what a microscope is. They find M in the index (or list), and see that beside "microscope" it has M 13. This means book M 13. It also has P. 424. This means page 424. They get the book with M 13 on the outside and find page 424. They are not surprised to see that the page is about microscopes. There are pictures on the page.

Ken reads, "A microscope is an instrument that sees little things." Dave reads, "A microscope is an instrument that magnifies objects."

"What does 'magnifies objects' mean?" Ken asks. Dave says, " 'Magnifies objects' means that it makes things look bigger." They read the page and look at the pictures. It makes them want to look through a microscope.

Dave has a friend who uses a microscope at his work. The two boys go to see him and ask to look through his microscope. He lets them do this and puts a drop of water from a pool on to a glass slide. Dave and Ken are surprised to see tiny living things in the drop of water.

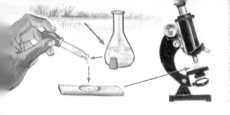

37

A frog, a whale and a lantern fish

Gail and Sandra are at the library. They look through the pages of an encyclopedia. They like animals and they want to find out more about them.

They see the picture of a tiny frog. It is a young tree frog. They are surprised that it is so very small. They read that it will grow larger, but not much.

Then they read about the blue whale. They know that whales are large, but this blue whale is huge. There is a good picture of one as it jumps out of the sea.

A young Western Tree Frog

The Blue Whale is the largest living animal

"They are so different," says Gail. "Yes," says Sandra. "The frog is so tiny, and the blue whale is so huge."

The girls turn some more pages. "Look at this," says Gail. "This lantern fish lives deep down in a part of the sea where it is dark. It has its own light, that is why it is called a lantern fish. A lantern has a light."

A Lantern Fish has its own lights

Kangaroos

Sandra reads about kangaroos. She knows that the mother kangaroos carry their young in a pouch on the body. She wants to know more.

She learns that kangaroos come from Australia, and the islands near Australia. There are different kinds of kangaroo. The very small ones are only about as large as a cat, but the largest ones are bigger than a man. All the mother kangaroos carry their young in a pouch on the body.

They have four legs. Two of the four legs are small, and the other two – the back legs – are very large and strong. They have long tails. These tails are also large and strong.

Kangaroos do not like to fight. They fight only when afraid or angry. When they move, they jump along. They can move quickly and they can jump high with their strong back legs.

Kangaroos have been living on earth for millions of years. Skeletons found of the kangaroos of long, long ago show that they were much larger than the ones here now.

Fighting

Jumping

41

Koalas

"Look at these lovely little things!" says Gail. She shows Sandra a book with a picture of two small animals, a mother with a young cub on her back. They are in a tree.

"Yes," says Sandra. "They are lovely. What are they? Are they bears? Tell me what it says in the book."

"They are koalas," says Gail, as she looks at the page. "It is a mother koala and her young cub. They live in Australia."

She goes on to read that the mother koala has a pouch on her body to carry her cub. When the cub gets bigger she likes to carry it on her back. The koala is a small animal with four legs, and its tail is very small. Some people call it a koala bear, but it is not a bear.

"It looks as if it would make a lovely pet," says Sandra.

"No," says Gail. "It is natural for the koala to live in trees. You could not keep it in the house."

Living at the bottom of the sea

"I didn't know that men could live at the bottom of the sea for a long time," says Sandra to Gail. "Look at this picture. It shows something like a house at the bottom of the sea. It says five men can live and work in it."

"Why do they do it?" asks Gail.

Sandra reads and then says, "They want to know more about the sea, and the things that live in the sea. They want to find out more about the land under the water. Most of the surface of the earth is under the water. In years to come, there may be many more people on earth. Men may want to get more food from the sea."

"Yes," says Gail. "More people, more food. More oil and gas too. We have a lot of oil and gas now, but we want more."

Sandra says, "Yes, we want more food, more oil and more gas."

"Look at that cage," says Gail. "I can read *shark cage* on the picture. The shark cage is to keep sharks away from the men. Sharks are dangerous."

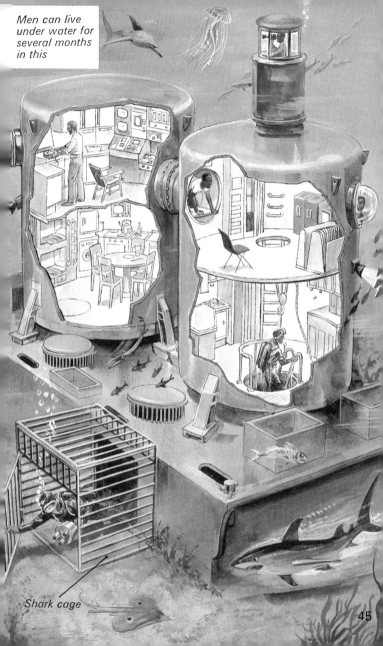

Men can live under water for several months in this

Shark cage

45

Electricity

Barry and Dave look through a new book at the library to learn about electricity. They are surprised to find out that there are tiny electric currents in our bodies. The electric currents inside us are very small, but we have to have them to live. There is a small current of electricity in most things.

Some kinds of fish have a lot of electricity in them. They use the electricity to help them to fight and to get food. The living things with most electricity in their bodies are electric eels. You can get a big electric shock from an electric eel.

You see natural electricity when there is lightning in a storm. Lightning can hurt or kill you. A strong electric shock can be very dangerous. So we must be careful in a storm when we see lightning.

Men make electricity to help them at home or at work.

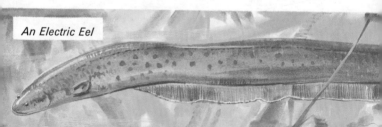

An Electric Eel

Lightning is electricity in nature

Most people use man-made electricity every day in many different ways. But we have to be careful with anything that uses it. No one wants to get an electric shock from lightning or from man-made electricity.

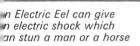
An Electric Eel can give an electric shock which can stun a man or a horse

More about electricity

The boys read in their new book how electricity is made.

One of the best ways to make electricity is to use a magnet and a coil of wire. You put the magnet inside the coil of wire and keep turning the magnet. The magnet must turn quickly inside the coil of wire. The more quickly it turns the more electricity will be made.

Coil of wire

Magnet

If you do this you have made an electric generator.

The magnet and coil of wire could be so small that you could hold the little generator in one hand. This would make only a very little electricity. Or a generator could be as large as a house. This would make a very strong current which could give heat and light for a great many homes, schools and other large buildings.

You must not fly a kite near electric wires or you may get an electric shock. You must not fly a kite in a storm, when there is lightning about, for this is dangerous, too.

Water turns the magnets in this large electric generator

49

Can you read the words when you cover the pictures?

1   The children are at the library.
2   Inside the earth rock has melted.
3   In an earthquake the earth shakes.
4   Coral is found only in warm seas.
5   Columbus sailed to the West Indies.
6   You can see the Kaieteur Falls from the cliffs.
7   Trinidad sends asphalt to Britain.
8   Aluminium does not rust.
9   Dinosaurs lived on earth long ago.
10 Children always ask questions.
11 This ship sank to the bottom.
12 He won the race.
13 A humming bird has lovely feathers.
14 Any kangaroo can jump well.
15 This instrument is a microscope.
16 Koalas come from Australia.
17 A shark is dangerous.
18 An electric eel can give a shock.
19 Lightning is natural electricity.
20 You can make an electric generator with a magnet and a coil of wire.

51

Words new to the series used in this book

Page

4-5 library books borrow Lyn best story Ray

6-7 much pictures rock metal melted

8-9 volcano lava opening surface shows cools

10-11 springs heated pipes

12-13 earthquake part shakes happens damage buildings few

14-15 coral made skeletons tiny added different garden

16 only warm glass

18 eels river Atlantic Ocean Sargasso seaweed years

20 stories told said did

22 Christopher Columbus sailed Spain West Indies thought

24 Kaieteur Guyana than Niagara five cliffs pool

26-27 Pitch Lake Trinidad asphalt road natural Britain

Page

29 village sank ago w feathers worshippe spirit angry sink

30 aluminium bauxite light rust found so also

32 footprint dinosaur millions any huge beside

34 questions answers encyclopedia collec knowledge index li page

36 microscope surprise instrument magnifie objects drop living

38-39 frog whale lantern young blue largest

40 kangaroos carry pouch body Austral four tails

42 koalas lovely cub bear

44 may food oil gas to cage shark

46 electricity new electric currents sho lightning storm care

48 magnet coil wire turning generator

Total number of words 144

WADE

If you can see or test the depth of the water, wade until you can reach with a stick or your coat but *ONLY if there is someone there to hold you. DON'T* try to swim.

ROW

If there is a boat nearby which you can safely manage, use it. Don't try to get the person into the boat — tow him to the bank.

GO

Go for help as quickly as you can if you can't reach, throw, wade or row.

Acknowledgments
The author and publishers wish to acknowledge the help of the
following in the preparation of this book: Balcan Engineering Ltd
(BELL Lifelines); Beaufort Air-Sea Equipment Ltd; British Seagull;
Helly-Hansen (UK) Ltd; PGL Adventure Ltd; Plain Sailing
(Kidderminster); Solihull Metropolitan Borough Council Swimming
Baths; Solihull Swimming and Water Polo Club; Stratford-upon-
Avon Rowing Club; Sydenham-Notcutt Ltd; and West Midland
Sailboarding Club. Additional photographic material was supplied
by: page 28, Tim Clark; pages 52, 53, Peter Hadfield; pages 4,
33, Kevin Rook; pages 5, 6, 7, 12, 43, Seaphot Ltd.

First edition

© LADYBIRD BOOKS LTD MCMLXXXI

Water Safety

by ROBERT BIRCH

photographs by
JOHN HEMMING
illustrations by
KATHY LAYFIELD

Ladybird Books Loughborough

This is called
white water
canoeing. Those
who take part
must practise
for a long time
before they are
allowed to race
in conditions
such as these.

On warm days, many people like to water ski.
A powerful boat with two drivers is advisable
and the skier should be equipped with a specially
strong buoyancy aid.

*A combination of strength and skill is needed to achieve this
exciting result. (WARNING Never swim where water skiing
or windsurfing is taking place).*

The British Water Ski Federation
163 Euston Road, London NW1
will give advice.

Ocean racing is very exciting.
The crews of these boats practise sailing as a team
so that they can do everything quickly and safely.

Some people like to go *under* the water, either scuba diving or deep sea diving.
They all start by joining clubs and, even when trained, dive in groups.
There are strict safety and training rules.

The British Sub Aqua Club
163 Euston Road, London NW1
will help you.

The sports that take place in or on water are all very adventurous, and the people that take part must be good swimmers and trained in water safety.

Water is beautiful to look at and great fun to play in, but it can be dangerous. Here, Eddie and Pam have found a safe place to play, and their Mum and Dad are close by.

9

Fish can live in water because they have gills which can take the oxygen out of water.

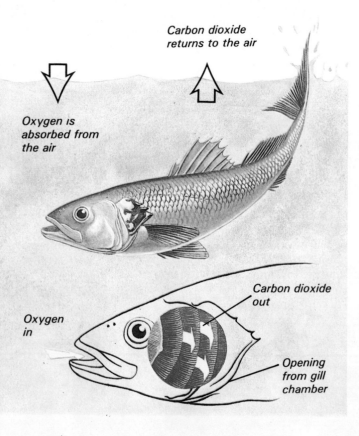

Carbon dioxide returns to the air

Oxygen is absorbed from the air

Carbon dioxide out

Oxygen in

Opening from gill chamber

Our lungs can only breathe air and we can't live for more than a few minutes without it.

Some animals, like whales, breathe air but can live happily for an hour or more without breathing.

There are other animals which breathe air and can stay under water for a long time such as seals and dolphins.

The Blue Whale —
the largest mammal that
has ever lived

You could not stay under water for more than a few minutes unless you had special equipment.

Without this equipment, you need to keep your head above water.

You must learn to keep your head above water in case you fall in by accident. These children are learning to 'tread water'.

Mums and Dads
Never let children play by water unsupervised. Always make sure you know where your children are, and that they are with a responsible grown-up.

This river is deep and the current is strong.
If Pam fell in, she could be swept away.
If you are walking near water, make sure you
are well away from the edge.

Mums and Dads

Banks can suddenly collapse or be very slippery. Make your children walk in front, where you can keep an eye on them, and make them walk well away from the edge.

The river on the left looks clean and pleasant but it might be just as poisonous as this pond.

Nobody would want to swim or paddle in this. Never jump into water unless you know it is safe.

Mums and Dads

Make sure your children know why it is dangerous to paddle or swim in rivers or ponds. Deep pools and strong currents can take them by surprise, and polluted water can make them ill.
Make sure too that any lakes,

rivers and streams that your children paddle in are free of pollution. Even though a stream may be some distance from a farm, for example, you cannot rely on the fact that sheepdip or herbicides have dispersed.

This dog is very well trained.
He walks at heel quietly,
and does not pull Pam along.
If your dog isn't well trained, he can easily pull
you into the water.

These children will enjoy their day out.
They can paddle with their sandals on and will
wash their hands in clean water before eating.

Mums and Dads

Broken glass or rusty metal can give children nasty cuts. Let them play in old sandals or plimsolls. Take a face-cloth and some water to wash their hands before they eat.

Never allow children to paddle or swim in canals or rivers on which boats navigate. Besides being particularly dangerous it is an offence against the byelaws on most navigable water.

Eddie's friends love sliding on these frozen puddles.
They know that they must not walk on the frozen pond because the ice is too thin and would break.

Mums and Dads
Never allow children to play on their own near a pond when it is frozen over unless you know the ice is thick enough for skating. The temptation to walk on the ice is too great.

If you had fallen through the ice like this dog, you might die of cold before you could be rescued, or you might be pulled under the ice by the flow of water.

It's fun to look at the fish in the goldfish pond, but don't go too near the edge.
If you fell and hit your head on a stone, you could drown, even if the water wasn't very deep.

Eddie and Pam have a water butt in their garden.
It has a cover over it.

Mums and Dads

Make sure that any water container is covered. Do not even leave water in a bucket where there is a very young child who could reach it. A bucket of hot water is still more dangerous.

21

Eddie and Pam love to help in the kitchen.

Do you ever spill water on the floor?
It can make you slip. Always wipe it up.

Mums and Dads

Never leave the kettle lead where a child can reach to pull it or trip over it.

Remember that wet floors can be very slippery. When the floor has just been washed, it is a good idea to tie a piece of string from the door handle across the doorway so that children won't rush in. Always wipe up spillages immediately.

Eddie and Pam sometimes stay with their Granny. Her bathroom was very old-fashioned, but she has had it modernised.

All the lights in this bathroom have cord pull-switches. The bath has grab-handles, and a non-slip mat in the bottom.

Apart from central heating radiators or heated towel rails, the best alternative is a bulb which provides both heat and light.

Mums and Dads

If your bathroom has a wall switch for the light, change it for a ceiling mounted pull-switch. Electric heaters should be mounted high on the wall, well away from the bath out of harm's way, with the switch outside the bathroom. An electric shaver should be used in the bathroom only if you have a special shaver socket. Never take any other electrical appliance into the bathroom.

When you run your bath, always run the cold tap
first, then warm the water by running the hot tap,
so that you don't scald yourself.

Gran and Grandad paid for Eddie and Pam to have swimming lessons at the baths.

They enjoyed learning to swim and later they went to life-saving classes to earn their life-saving awards.

Mums and Dads

Make sure your children are taught to swim. Go to the baths with them and encourage them to swim really well. Make it a regular family outing. Start them young — two or three years old is ideal. If babies of about eighteen months old are introduced to the water, they are unlikely to have any fear of it and may swim naturally.

0.9 m

Eddie and Pam have taken their Water Safety Award.
Now Eddie is working for his Junior Swimmer Award.

Awards start with an easy test and go on to cover Water Safety, speed, distance, life-saving and personal survival.

At the swimming baths, safe behaviour is essential.

Do not run or play chasing games.

Do not shout or shriek.

NEVER PUSH PEOPLE INTO THE WATER.

MAKE SURE THAT THE WATER IS DEEP ENOUGH AND CLEAR OF OTHER SWIMMERS BEFORE YOU JUMP OR DIVE IN.

If you wear goggles, learn how to use them properly.

Eddie and Pam belong to the Junior Swimming Club at their baths.

They love playing water games and learning life saving.

Mums and Dads

Let your children swim regularly and learn both breast and crawl strokes really well. Let them become completely 'at home' in the water.

Goggles can be dangerous. Only buy those carrying the British Standards Institution kite mark.

Water sports are great fun — especially when you learn your chosen sport properly. You must be able to swim at least 50 metres wearing sports shirt and shorts.

You should know how to 'tread water' and float on your back.

Wear the right clothing (see page 47).

Get the right equipment and keep it in good order (see pages 48-49).

Do not drop rubbish.

Broken glass can cut you and others.

A plastic bag can stop a boat's engine, which might be dangerous.

Litter is unpleasant.

Mums and Dads

Encourage your children to take up water sports but make sure they are taught properly. Never let them go alone — there should always be somone who is competent keeping an eye on them.

Never buy anything until you are sure it is everything the salesman says, and get unbiased advice. You can learn a lot from magazines which specialise in each water sport.

Look out for the British Standards kite mark and the BS followed by a number.

Eddie and his Dad have gone to a sailing club to find out if they could learn to sail.
They learn lots of useful things.
Eddie's Dad is pleased that they can both learn to sail without buying a boat!

Mums and Dads

There are many sailing clubs, local Education Authority and private sailing schools where tuition reaches an approved standard. The Royal Yachting Association, Victoria Way, Woking will advise you.

Eddie is learning how to paddle a kayak properly.
He finds it isn't as easy as it looks!

He knows he must always wear a lifejacket and
a helmet.
He will learn how to make the kayak go straight.
He will learn how to capsize, and recover.
When he is very good at canoeing, he will enjoy
rolling right over and surfacing again.

ROWING

Rowing is a very old water sport.

The boats (called *shells*) are very expensive.

There can be one, two, four, or even eight in the boat.

They go very fast.

Everyone in the boat must work as a team, which takes a lot of practice.

You must be a good swimmer to survive if you capsize.

Wear warm clothes and strong, comfortable shoes and socks!

It is best to row only when a trainer is present or a rescue boat is available.

The Amateur Rowing Association
6 Lower Mall, London W6 9DJ
will help with advice.

WINDSURFING

Windsurfing (or boardsailing) will make your arms ache at first, but you can learn very quickly if you are taught by an expert.

The right clothing is important for safety.

This windsurfer is wearing a wet suit. It will keep her warm both in and out of the water. It will *not* keep her dry. It will *not* keep her afloat. She needs a buoyancy aid as well.

The UK Boardsailing Association,
19 Hartland Road, London NW1
can help you.

FISHING

Eddie's Dad goes fishing for trout and salmon. This is called *game fishing*.

Eddie has a rod and line with a float and sinker. This is called *coarse fishing*.

If *you* go fishing, make sure you follow all the safety rules shown opposite.

The boys below are coarse fishing.

Mums and Dads
Never let children go fishing unless you know where they are going and that they are with someone responsible. Tell them what time they must be back, and see that they are properly equipped. Remember that hook injuries can cause tetanus – seek medical advice.

SAFETY RULES WHEN FISHING

Never go fishing alone.

Go with a friend and stay within sight of a grown-up.

Always tell your Mum where you are going.

Stop fishing and go home well before dark.

Don't go fishing unless you can swim.

Walk carefully near the water.

Don't run – you might trip or slip into the water.

Don't stand too close to the water, especially on rocks at the seaside. A big wave could knock you into the sea.

Always find a comfortable place to sit.

It's a good idea to tie a string to a tree, and fix it to your belt.

Never fish from a muddy bank where you might slip.

If your line gets tangled, don't go into the water unless you can see it is shallow. Call a grown-up for help.

Keep well away from other anglers.

Don't walk behind an angler – the hook flies back when he casts and might hurt you.

Be careful of the hook. If it sticks in you, let the wound bleed for a few seconds. If it goes right in, don't try to get it out – go for help.

Only go fishing in a boat when there is a grown-up with you. Fish sitting down and don't move about.

Always wear a buoyancy aid or lifejacket.

Never wear rubber boots in a boat.

Eddie and Pam went on a boat trip. They wore their lifejackets except when they went into the cabin for tea.

The boat went quite slowly so that it did not make big waves.

In small boats you should always sit on the seats properly. If you fell out of this boat you might go under the boat straight to the propeller.

Keep your fingers inside the boat.

Be careful to keep your head down when going under low bridges.

NATIONAL CODE FOR BATHERS

Never bathe when the RED FLAG flies.
Never bathe where there is a red danger notice.
Bathe between the red and yellow flags.
If there are no flags, ask if bathing is safe.

Bathe where most people are bathing.
Never bathe alone.
Swim in line with the beach.
Don't stay in the water too long.
Don't go into the water too soon after eating.

Take care of Mum and Dad
– make sure they follow
the bathers' code too!

39

In the summer holidays, Eddie and Pam's friends go with their Mums and Dads to the seaside.

They love to go swimming on the beach. They keep away from the rocks where the sign says DANGER, and play on the other rocks which are not dangerous.

Mums and Dads

When you go to a beach look for any warning signs, and follow their advice.

Only bathe where there are others bathing.

If there are red-and-yellow flags, the beach between them will be supervised by a lifeguard, and you should bathe there.

Find out where the nearest telephone is in case you might need it quickly.

Find out whether the tide is coming in or going out, and what time will be high or low tide.

Always keep an eye on young children, and stay close to them when they are in the water.

40

DANGER
FROM
FALLING ROCKS
KEEP AWAY

41

At the seaside never play on an inflatable toy or boat unless there is a grown-up to hold on to it for you.

Mums and Dads

Wind or tide can quickly carry an inflatable boat or airbed out to sea. Never put an airbed on the water.

Inflatable toys and boats must have a strong rope all round *and* must be held at all times.

It's fun to go looking for shells when the tide is out, but you can be cut off from the main beach very quickly.

Keep a look-out all the time.

Never dive or jump into water unless a grown-up has checked that it is safe to do so.

Snorkelling is fun, but always remember to keep the tube vertical.

Swill the face mask out with water before you start, and breathe through your mouth.

LIFE-SAVING EQUIPMENT

You often see lifebuoys near water. Sometimes they are red and white — sometimes they are orange.

This is so that they can be seen easily in the water.

44

Eddie is surprised at how heavy the lifebuoy is.
Even the lifeguard cannot throw it very far.
There is no need to get into the ring in the
water.
It has ropes to hold, and a rope to pull it to
safety.

45

Where there are signs telling you about special dangers, always follow the advice given – the notice has only been put there to draw attention to the danger.

Sometimes there are throwing lines by the water or in a large boat. These lines can be thrown to save someone much further away than a lifebuoy can reach.

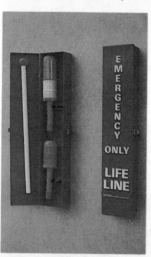

When throwing a lifeline, remember to hold the free end tightly.

YOUR OWN LIFE-SAVING EQUIPMENT

If you go onto the water in any kind of boat, you *must* wear either a *Lifejacket* or a *Buoyancy Aid*.

A *Lifejacket* will keep you afloat with your head above water even if you are injured or unconscious.

A *Buoyancy Aid* will help you to float but you will have to keep your head above water.

Here are four types of Lifejacket:
1 Some are fully filled ready for use.
2 Some are half filled with buoyant foam.
3 Some are worn flat and need to be inflated by mouth or by a small gasbottle.
4 Children under seven need special lifejackets.

Although the first type sometimes gets in the way, it is the safest.
The second type is less noticeable to wear, and keeps you afloat while you blow it up fully.

Buoyancy Aids are lighter and less bulky in use.

Eddie and his Dad decided to get buoyancy aids for when they start sailing.

The assistant told them all about the different makes, and let them try them on to choose the ones which fitted best.

She made sure that Eddie's was a good fit.

If your buoyancy aid is too big, it will come up over your face; you would be better without it.

Straps under your legs will stop this happening.

Mums and Dads

Lifejackets are made to British Standard 3595. Buoyancy Aids are made to a specification of the Ship and Boat Builders' *National Federation (SBBNF). Don't buy either unless they comply with these standards.*

If you are taken out in a boat, here is a check-list of equipment you might need.
Can you think why you might need these things?

Warm clothes; waterproof clothes, boating shoes; anchor and rope; distress flares; oars; enough fuel for the engine; tools for the engine; torch; lifejackets; spare rope; waterproof wrist watch; radio (for weather forecast); packed lunch and tea.

LEARN BASIC WATER SAFETY

Watch out for possible dangers, but if you do fall into the water –

Try to take a deep breath as you fall; hold your breath until your head is above water; try to keep your eyes open; get hold of anything that might support you; shout for help; take a deep breath and try to stand up – the water may not be as deep as you thought; take off wellingtons or heavy shoes, but not other clothes; keep calm, and signal for help by holding *one* arm in the air; if you were in a boat, stay with the boat even if it is upside-down. Do *not* swim away from it; if you are in a river, swim across the current, not against it.

To save others

Keep calm and *think*;
shout for help if there are grown-ups nearby;
try to REACH with a stick or whatever you can
find;
take off your coat or shirt and reach with that;
keep down low so that you don't fall in;
if you can't reach, THROW something which
floats, or one end of a rope if you can find one;
only go into the water if you can WADE to reach
with a stick and if there is someone to hold you;
don't try to help by swimming;
if you are on your own and can't reach or throw
something, run as quickly as you can for help.

THE RESCUE SERVICES

If you think someone needs help, go to a telephone. Dial 999.

If you are inland, ask for the POLICE.

At the seaside, ask for the COASTGUARD.

Tell them what has happened.
Answer all their questions calmly.
Don't be afraid to say, "I don't know" if you really don't.

The Coastguard can call on a number of SEARCH AND RESCUE teams.